Yemi Odunfa

Don't Tell Daddy What Happened in Lagos

A Play

Illustrations by Segun Akeredolu

Podsixteen

For Dad and Mum

Stephen and Victoria

Acknowledgment

Her name is Joy. She lights up my world. Thank you for everything.

To our boys, N and S, anything is possible. Never stop dreaming.

To my dear siblings, there aren't many things better than the sum of us.

To my family, friends, writing community, and editing team, thank you for encouraging me to write again.

To the reader

This is a story about many things.
I hope that within all its meanderings, you find your
one thing.

CAST

Yomi Oye
First born. A Pastor. Overbearing personality with extreme ideas of masculinity.

Oyin Oye
Second born. Tender-hearted with a loveable personality.

Kike Oye
Last born. Happy-go-lucky teenager. She is an undergraduate and presently five months pregnant.

Mrs Oye
Mother of the trio. She is a quick-witted, no-nonsense-taking realist.

Amy Antar
Intern. Personal assistant to Yomi.

Stephen
Oyin's boyfriend. He is not physically present throughout the play.

STAGE

The set is an expansive modern living room. The design is minimalist with potted flowers dotting strategic locations.

Separate exit doors lead into a kitchen and a bathroom. A small flight of stairs by the side leads upstairs into bedrooms.

I'm trying hard not to panic, but what if...

SCENE ONE: LOST

Oyin is pacing with two mobile phones which she dials into repeatedly. Kike sits casually on a lounge chair, watching her sister's erratic activity.

Oyin I'm trying hard not to panic, but what if . . . what if something terrible has happened to him? It's past midnight, and I still can't get through to any of his phones!

Kike *(Appears unflustered)* I think you need to calm down; you have been pacing up and down all night. Our brother will be fine. Have some faith . . . in God, the universe, or whatever.

Oyin We haven't heard anything from him since he left the house yesterday! I think I've exhausted all my patience! *(With furtive activity on the phone)* I'll call Stephen. We'll drive to the church office and make enquiries at all the police stations and hospitals along the route.

Kike Yomi can take care of himself. It's not the first time he's returned home late.

Oyin *(With a huff)* It is the third time he has disappeared this week, without anyone knowing his whereabouts! Where does he go off to? What is he running away from?

Kike Everything will be fine, trust me. *(Pats the sofa next to her)* Come sit down with me.

Oyin You know, your calmness is both infuriating as well as suspicious. Kike, do you know where Yomi is?

Kike No, no, honestly, I'm just as clueless right now as you are! *(Suddenly appears briefly pensive)* I think I just felt the baby kick. Do you want to feel it?

Oyin sits next to Kike who takes her hands gently. Kike helps her feel her tummy and there is a moment of awe.

Oyin *(Excitedly)* Oh my God; yes I felt it! Oh, Kike!

Kike *(Briefly melancholic)* It is precious, isn't it?

Oyin *(Reaches for her hand and speaks more seriously)* Have you made up your mind about keeping the baby?

Kike I haven't changed my mind.

Oyin *(Gently)* You know you can trust me, Kike. Do you . . . *(Asks cautiously)* Do you not know who the father is?

She is briefly quiet.

Kike It doesn't matter.

Oyin (With gentle disapproval) What about Mum? You haven't told her about the baby. She has a right to know that her daughter is pregnant.

Kike My body, my decision, my prerogative. . . isn't it?

Oyin I love you, Kike, but you are not being very reasonable! You simply cannot get pregnant, carry a baby for nine months, keep everything hush, deliver the baby, and then just make it vanish! Lies and secrets never amount to any good.

Kike I'm not lying. I'm just choosing what not to disclose. I am picking my battles, and it has worked well for me so far. A little bit more perseverance — even if it means remaining cooped up in this house for another couple of months; the baby will be gone, and everyone's lives can return to normal. Besides, you know that if Mummy finds out, she will literally kill me.

Oyin Yes, I know.

Kike *(With a dry laugh)* And you consent to my slaughter?

Oyin Of course not literally . . . but having a baby and what you choose to do about it is a life changing decision! You need all the guidance and support you can get. I really think you need to get Mum involved.

Kike *(Quietly)* If dad were around . . . I would have . . . I would have told him everything. *(Brief pause)* He would have been so disappointed . . .

Oyin We all make mistakes, Kike. Daddy knew that. He used to say, "it is not our mistakes that define us, it is the choices we make out of them." I'm sure he is cheering you on, praying that you find strength and common sense to make the right decision.

Kike It will be one year this weekend since Dad left us. It's a good thing he is no longer around to see the utter mess some of us have turned out to be. One first born Man of God who seems to be going through a midlife crisis, one pregnant teenage daughter, and, of course, his perfect middle child. It's not exactly the esteemed legacy of faith Dad always wanted.

Oyin *(Musingly)* It's funny how so much can change in one year. When the centre can no longer hold, things fall apart.

There is a sound of incoming footsteps; the two ladies perk their heads quickly towards the sounds. An infuriated Yomi marches in with a hesitant Amy following behind her.

Oyin It's Yomi! Oh, thank God! Where have you been?

Yomi heads towards the bedroom without acknowledging his sisters' presence. He has a slight stagger indicative of inebriation. Amy waits a small distance away.

Oyin stands and attempts to block Yomi's path.

Oyin Have you been drinking?

Yomi *(Attempts unsuccessfully to sidestep her)* Oyin, I'm not in the best mood right now so . . . just clear out of my way!

Oyin persists and restrains his movement.

Oyin You've kept us both awake all night! The least you will do is offer an explanation. Where were you? You look like a mess, and you stink of alcohol.

Yomi *(Incredulously)* I don't owe you any explanation — you're not my mother!

Amy *(Speaks with professional calmness)* The Pastor was arrested. I got a call from the church office to sort out his bail release. He has a pending case at the police station, but we should be able to resolve that within a few days.

Oyin Arrested? What do you mean arrested? What did you do?

Yomi *(Cynically)* I was out . . . at a party and had a little bit of alcohol — end of story.

Oyin *(Ridiculously)* You were out drinking at two a.m.? What were you thinking?

Yomi I'm not having this conversation right now, Oyin, but thank you for waiting for me. I have a Church leadership meeting in a few hours; I need to get some rest.

Oyin No, no, you're not going to sleep! We've been worried sick! This family was placed under your care after . . . after Dad passed. We're supposed to look out for each other here in Lagos but look around at this mess! Kike is pregnant at age nineteen — with circumstances shrouded in unfathomable secrecy!

You on the other hand, are just doing as you please — from late night drinking escapades to police stations at two a.m.! This is the third time this week! Have you forgotten who you are, Pastor Yomi? Our father was the Archbishop of the Church! If Mum knew the real state of this family right now, she'd literally have a heart attack!

Yomi Well, Mum is not here, is she? For once, please quit with the preaching! This prim and perfect daughter act is starting to get annoying!

Oyin Yomi! Call me whatever you wish — frankly, I don't care. What I do care about are the consequences of your recklessness.

Kike I am not interested in this family becoming tomorrow's front-page news story — about all your private parties and arrest. Imagine the headlines:

'*National Parish Pastor, son of the late Archbishop, arrested at a late-night club party.*' The gossip blogs will love that!

Yomi *(Defensively)* I wasn't arrested; I was just being detained.

Kike Why were you detained?

Yomi Mind your business! I am entitled, as much as everyone is, to some time out. It was a private party. Nobody except the very small number of people at the venue knew about the party or the issue with the police. There isn't going to be any gossip news.

Oyin Answer her question! Why were you detained?

Yomi *(He starts to march off)* I've had a long day; I need some rest.

Amy Ermm. . . excuse me . . .

Yomi Your work is done here, Amy; you may leave.

Amy *(Attempts to mask her discontentment)* Yes, of course, Pastor — *(Brief pause)* — But can we have a word in private before I take my leave?

Yomi Say what you need to say quickly. My head is banging! *(Turning briefly to the two)* I don't think you two have met Amy. She is my new P.A. and interning as one of the Church's legal counsels. She joined the Parish just last month.

Kike Nice to meet you Amy . . . thank you for your help.

Yomi *(Impatiently)* Well, what is it, Amy?

Amy *(Rummages in her pocket)* I think we may have a problem . . . which I am worried could get out of hand.

Yomi *(With a tinge of irritation)* Can we discuss this at the Church later?

Amy I think it may be best that I let you know now. *(Seen fidgeting with her phone)* Someone has been sending me text messages since we left the station.

Yomi What messages?

Amy *(Hesitates briefly)* Photos. Pictures of you, from the club . . . It seems you were with a young girl.

Yomi *(Face visibly ashen)* What pictures? What are you talking about?

She hands Yomi her phone. He flicks through quickly and gasps.

Amy Do you know who she is? They are very compromising photos. These pictures can get you in a lot of trouble.

Kike Let me see!

Yomi Mind your business! *(Visibly shaken)* Who sent these to you?

Amy I don't know. I have tried to reach the sender but so far received no response.

Oyin *(Throws her hands up with frustration)* I have warned you, Yomi. You cannot continue to indulge in these liberties. You are soon going to be part of the Church senior leadership!

Kike Everything you do, every mistake you make is newsworthy for gossip and mockery. You no longer have a private life!

Oyin If you have no intention of taking the ministry seriously, you should hand it over to someone else instead of burning the whole thing to the ground!

Yomi I would gladly hand it over to anyone! I didn't exactly have a choice in accepting this duty. Follow your father's steps to train at the Seminary to become a pastor, then set yourself apart till you are called to join the Vicarage — they said. Should I have declined Daddy's dying wishes?

Brief silence

Oyin Clearly, yes! But you are deflecting. That is not the issue here!

Yomi *(Hotly)* It is the issue! This, and everything else that makes this an issue is about my life and my freedom. It is my life being sacrificed on this altar of duty. All my life, I have toed the line — Bible school, ministry service, clergy work, and now this ordination. Let's be clear — I didn't ask for this!

Oyin *(Turns to Amy)* Can you help us manage this, Amy, before those pictures get out of control?

Amy *(Looks briefly to Yomi)* The thing is . . . the party was at an off-licence venue. These venues are intentionally out of reach from scrutiny.

Oyin I don't understand. What do you mean?

Amy Well . . . the party was inside a brothel.

Oyin A brothel! What do you mean?

Amy The Pastor was at a party, a sex party inside a brothel. There was a police raid — that's where he was arrested.

Oyin Oh my god, Yomi!

Amy Honestly, that is half of the problem. We can handle the arrest with the police, you know . . . The bigger problem is the girl. The person sending the text messages is alleging that the girl he was seen with — the one in the pictures, is apparently underage. She is just a teenager. Did you know this?

Yomi How was I supposed to know her age?! She wasn't dressed like a teenager!

Yomi's phone rings out. He ignores it.

Amy Do you want your sisters to see the photos — so that everyone understands the gravity of this situation?

Yomi dumps both phones aside with enraged annoyance.

Yomi This has nothing to do with my sisters!

Oyin What were you doing with a teenager, Yomi?

Amy The thing is anyone in the club could have taken the photos. We don't know how many people have these photos.

Yomi *(Hotly)* I said the party was in a private room! It was a private party! Nobody is supposed to have those photos!

Oyin Yomi, why were you in a private room with teenage girls — in a brothel?

Yomi *(Hotly)* I heard your question the first, second, and third time! Can you just let me think! I don't know how this thing got leaked!

Oyin You have had more than enough time to think! I mean, surely you must have considered your choices before you went off gallivanting! The fact that you needed to take precaution to conceal your whereabouts — did that not strike you that your decisions were morally deficient?

Yomi I don't owe you or anyone any explanations.

Oyin You are a pastor! You are about to be ordained Right Reverend and someone has photos of you with teenage prostitutes at a brothel! This ridiculous situation could easily escalate into a complete train wreck — for you, this family, and the church? What do you think the Diocese would do if they saw these pictures?

Yomi's phone rings again. He ignores it.

Amy It is not in my place to comment on your private life, but you are the face of the ministry, the largest Diocese in the country. If these photos get out into the public, you will be roasted all over tabloid blogs until it becomes front page news and then you will be arrested. You will destroy the credibility of the Diocese and the Church.

Kike Let's not get over dramatic. I'm sure you can fix this. Can't you make it go away with some legal bamboozling?

Oyin You can't just damage control everything! I mean, does anyone not tell the truth anymore? God help me, I don't want to know, but . . . give me that phone!

There is a frenzied scramble for the phone between Oyin and Yomi. Oyin finally gets it, scrolls through and gasps. She lowers herself into the sofa, clearly shocked.

Oyin Jesus Christ, Yomi! What is this? What is this?

There is prolonged silence.

Amy You see that it is very incriminating stuff. You need to make this go away very quickly before these photos progress into an ugly blackmail. I hate to say this, but whatever they ask for, pay it, and start thinking about how to get your acts and stories straight before this gets out of your hands completely.

Oyin You want the church to pay hush money! What do you think will happen after you *bribe* this person? Do you think they'd really delete the pictures and make it go away? The leverage is in their hands. A blackmail can go on forever, with no reasonable conclusion. The narrative will get even more ridiculous when it is discovered you were cooperating and sending money!

Kike It could also all just blow itself out, couldn't it? Most people don't really care about anyone's private lives these days, do they?

Amy It's not just about what people think. Soliciting a prostitute — and more so, a minor under eighteen — is a criminal offence.

Yomi I know what the law says!

Oyin *(Hotly)* What about the Church? Do you know what the Church says . . . what the Bible says? Which laws precisely are you even concerned about? The girls barely look fifteen, Yomi!

Yomi I was drunk, okay! I had a bit too much to drink!

Oyin Clearly enough to lose all your clothes — you are stark naked in that picture!

Amy You can't argue with photo evidence, and you can't preach your way out of it. You will need a very convincing argument to manage the implications if this gets out there. These photos could damage all your reputation and credibility.

Yomi lowers himself slowly into a chair.

Kike I think we have all said enough. Give the Pastor some space.

Brief silence

Amy I will need to let the Diocese know about this, Pastor. The Church will need to start thinking about damage-control options.

Yomi The Diocese does not need to know anything about this! I can sort this out. I will sort this out myself.

Yomi's phone rings again. He finally rummages in his pocket and pulls it out.

Yomi *(Appearing very frazzled)* It's Mum! *(He lets the phone ring unanswered while he paces about)*

Oyin Aren't you going to answer her call?

Yomi Of course not! I can't deal with that woman right now.

Oyin You can't just ignore Mummy's call! She wouldn't normally call at this time. You should speak with her — check that she is okay.

Yomi I said I can't deal with Mum right now. Is anyone not listening to me?

Oyin *(With impatience)* Give me the phone. I'll speak with her myself.

Oyin briskly collects the phone.

Kike If she asks for me, please tell her I am not available.

Oyin *(Speaks into it)* Hello, Mum. Is everything okay?

Listening pause
Mum, your line has a lot of background noise. I'm struggling to hear you. Where are you?

Listening pause

Airport? What airport? . . . Lagos? What do you mean? You didn't mention to any of us that you will be in town!

There is apparent rising panic among the siblings.

Who is picking you up? A taxi!

(She turns frantic eyes to her siblings) I am really confused . . . Mum, Mum, wait . . .

__The line cuts. Oyin pulls the phone away from her ear slowly with disbelief written all over on her face.__

Yomi *(With foreboding)* What was that about?

Oyin Mum is in town!

Kike *(With wide eyes of terror)* WHAT!

Oyin She says she's been trying to reach Yomi's phone without luck, so she has booked a taxi. She's heading down here from the airport. She says she will be here within two hours.

Yomi Oh my God!

SCENE ENDS.

SCENE TWO: LIES

Yomi It's the worst time for Mum to visit. Why didn't you try to discourage her?

Oyin What was I supposed to tell her? To turn around and catch a return flight to Port Harcourt?

Yomi You could have told her anything! Mum has no clue about the baby. She has no idea she's about to become a grandmother. She will literally have a heart attack!

Amy What about these pictures, Pastor? If the pictures go public, I doubt you will be able to hide the news or the implications from your mother, especially if she is in town.

Kike gets up abruptly.

Kike I'm not sticking around for this. Oyin, will you please help me pack up a few things. I'll find a hotel to stay at. I have intentionally stayed away from Mum since this *(motions at her belly).* I need more time. I just need three more months.

Oyin You are not going anywhere in your state! How do you intend on smuggling yourself with your belly into a hotel without being recognised? Who is going to pay for the hotel? Come on, Kike. It's time to put an end to this madness! Can you talk some sense into her, Yomi?

Kike No, Oyin, no! You must respect my decision on this. I simply do not want Mum involved right now. I could have aborted the baby, but I didn't. I am not keeping it and you know that is not going to happen if Mum gets involved. Nobody except Mum is in control of anything when she is involved.

Pause
If you can't pay for a hotel, I'll call a friend to stay with. Either way, I am not going to be here. Tell Mum I am out of town.
(Turns to Yomi)
Whatever is going on with you, you better be praying hard that it does not get out of control when Mum is around. Spare the woman any additional heartache.

Oyin What about this weekend — Dad's remembrance? Mum will not forgive you if you do not show up for your father's one-year memorial. There is no plausible excuse to justify your absence!

Kike Trust me; being around here isn't going to help anything or anyone. If you keep Mum busy whilst she's visiting, she'll hardly notice that I'm not here. Just find something to keep her distracted.

Oyin I'm not telling any more lies for you, Kike! Sort your mess out!

Amy *(Coughs briefly)* I can see that you all have a lot on your plate, so . . . I think I'll take my leave now.

Kike No . . . no . . . stay. I need some help . . . We need your help . . .
(Appearing thoughtful) We clearly have a few problems at hand. My mother cannot get involved with this pregnancy, at least not right now. Also, this situation with Yomi . . . The last thing we need right now is for my mother to arrive here to a ridiculous scandal of a lunatic posting naked pictures of her son online. It's my father's one-year remembrance this weekend. We can't deal with any unnecessary scandal right now. I need your help.

Amy *(Appears reluctant)* What do you need me to do exactly?

Kike *(Brief pause)* The text messages and the pictures — for the sake of this weekend and my mother's visit, can you just make them go away. *(Turns to Yomi)* You could pay money, or whatever this person is asking for — buy yourself some time to sort this out and control the narrative.

Yomi How? And where do you expect me to get money from?

Kike *(Paces about introspectively)* Here is my advice . . . and I am not oblivious to how ridiculous it is, but we have less than two hours before Mum knocks on the door! Yomi, you need damage control. You could introduce Amy to Mum and whoever cares to know, as your fiancée. Tell her you both just got engaged and give the impression that you are both planning to get married . . .

Yomi *(Laughs ridiculously)* How does that solve anything? Doesn't that in fact make things worse? I am suddenly engaged, yet there are random pictures circulating online of myself in compromising situations.

Amy Let's hear Kike out. You need credibility and positive publicity quickly. The problem is, so far you are a very single man whose moral character is about to be butchered, yet you are about to assume a church leadership role as Senior Bishop.

Kike Your good news engagement story will eclipse the scandal. You will then dismiss the photos as unintentional bad behaviour you got coerced into during your bachelor's party. You were drunk. It has never happened before and will never happen again. Isn't that so?

Yomi What exactly does this achieve?

Kike Distraction. What we need right now is a big distraction — to distract Mum from you, from me, and to contain the media chaos that is headed our way.

Oyin Your suggestion is to stage a pretend engagement and a wedding to preoccupy your mother and everyone else?

Kike Yes . . . yes. I think so.

Yomi *(Ridiculously)* You want me to pretend to be engaged to a woman I only met last week! Isn't that a bit far-fetched?

Kike *(With a tinge of irritation)* Would you rather get arrested and become the next trending blog gist or pretend to get married? It's just a smokescreen — an alibi of sorts. It will get Mum off your case and if the situation with the pictures gets out of hand, you can use Amy and the wedding as your fall back. *(Turns briefly to Amy)* You are happy to help, aren't you? It's just fake news.

Amy *(Hesitates briefly)* I mean, it does sound a bit extreme, but yes . . . that is my job really — to support however I can.

Kike Thank you. *(Turns to Yomi)* Go public with fake engagement news; it's just social media buffering. If somehow those pictures leak online and a damaging narrative about you starts to surface, just say the pictures were a harmless party that got out of hand. You are focused on your wedding and the Church and so you will not comment further. Images never scrub off the internet but hopefully the attention will die out eventually. Your wedding is the news everyone in the Church has been waiting for. It will eclipse any scandal.

Oyin *(Ridiculously)* Are you listening to yourself? Are you suggesting fixing one lie with a bigger lie?

Kike Do you have a better plan?

Oyin *(Ridiculously)* Yes, the truth! He is a Pastor, for god's sake! Just tell the truth — that is your basic job description! If these pictures are your truth, then you shouldn't be ashamed of owning them and showing some real repentance!

Kike The truth doesn't fix everything! *(Suddenly impassioned)* A randy Pastor and a pregnant teenage daughter — children of the late Archbishop Oye! Is that a truth you are ready to defend right now for the sake of this family's heritage?

Oyin Don't call him that! Don't you dare call him that!

The terse moment is captured by a brief pause.

Oyin *(Attempts to speak more calmly)* What does this lie fix?

Kike Time. It buys us time and space to resolve our lives. Call it reflection, repentance, or whatever. We need time to fix all of this. I also desperately need time and space.

Oyin I think it's a daft idea. You both need to simply tell the truth and own the consequences of your decisions.

Amy If you want my opinion, the truth cannot be an option right now — at least, not to the wider public. You have done very well to keep your private lives and secrets out of public scrutiny. If these stories get out, they will impact all of you. I have seen people and companies manage scandals and the approach is always the same. The church will need to survive the drama, and it will do that, by distancing itself from your family and your father's legacy. You all have a lot at stake. It sounds ridiculous, but I think it is worth considering Kike's idea. Buy yourselves some time and space to sort your lives out.

Yomi *(Contemplating)* What if . . . what if we allow the worst to happen? If all of these . . . these untidy stories go public and get out of hand, then our connections and obligations to Dad's ministry could effectively implode by itself, and everyone walks away free. It may be a small price to pay for freedom. We leave the ministry, and everyone gets a second chance at a normal private life.

Oyin You want to sacrifice the ministry, this family and all that dad has built all his life . . . to what end?

Yomi You were the one campaigning for truth!

Amy briefly looks to Kike.

Amy What you are suggesting is like detonating a wild cluster bomb and hoping to walk away unbruised. It is an unnecessary gamble. There will be consequences and casualties. We need Kike's plan.

Kike I am not keeping this child and I do not want Mum's involvement whatsoever. All I am asking for is only a little harmless white lie. Mum is desperate to marry one of us off. This plan will give us some needed emotional diversion for this weekend.

Oyin It is not a plan. It's a charade, a big, unnecessary lie.

Kike *(With a tinge of irritation)* Yes I can see that, but do you have a better plan that doesn't involve a train wreck confession?

Brief pause

Yomi Okay, fine! Kike, you can stay away — out of sight whilst Mum is here. We'll help you manage Mum. I agree that we'll need a reasonable distraction to justify you not being around this weekend; however, this engagement story will make more sense coming from Oyin.
(Turns to Oyin) Mummy approves of your relationship; she knows Stephen's family and she's exceptionally proud of her sensible second child. You're the better person to pull off this pretend wedding story.

Kike No Yomi, you are the one who needs to follow through with this!

Oyin I'm not telling any lies for you! I'm not going to be a part of any of this.

Kike Yomi, I really need YOU to stay with the plan, please! Mum will be here for just five nights. We only need to keep her busy for five nights.

Oyin How do you know she is staying just five nights?

Kike *(After a brief pause)* She needs to return in time for a wedding in Port Harcourt. All we need are neatly packaged lives to present when she gets here. When everything is over, we'll pull the strings and the whole thing will fall away neatly.

Oyin You can't stretch Mum's patience for five nights without you showing up in person Kike. You cannot tell lies to divert Mum's attention. That woman can hear a feather drop to the ground in the middle of a riot.

Kike Wedding preparations take a lot of time and concentration. To make it an even more compelling story, you can tell her you are planning for the engagement ceremony and the wedding in two weeks' time.

Amy Two weeks?

Oyin Nobody will ever believe that!

Yomi *(Appearing caught up on the idea)* If she does believe it, she'd put in everything to magic a wedding even if it's on three days' notice.

Oyin Are you listening to yourselves at all? What happens when Mum eventually finds out that we have all lied to her?

Yomi It's only a little lie.

Kike That's why we *can't* let her find out.

Yomi Coming from you, Oyin, she won't have any doubts or suspicions.

Oyin It's not a little lie; it's a very big lie! What if she starts calling her friends and the rest of our family to announce the good news and invite them to this imaginary wedding?

Kike We'll let her. Let her think about the invitations, the shopping, the whole preparation for a *real* wedding. We need as much excitement as possible to keep Mum disengaged from the real situation of things.

Yomi Don't overthink it; it's only for a few days. When Mum leaves and everything settles, we'll call it off and say you postponed the wedding. I think the idea has prospects.

Oyin It has prospects for a first-class disaster! You're both acting as if it's the end of the world. It's our *mother* coming to visit! So, what if you're pregnant; the mistake is already done — she's not going to kill you!

Kike I know I've asked for a lot of crazy things before and this might as well be the wildest, but please, I need to sort this pregnancy out myself as quietly as possible. Oyin is not going to consider it; can you just stick with the original plan. I need you, Yomi, to pull this off. All I'm asking for is time. Just help me distract Mum and buy me some time to take care of this quietly.

Yomi You know my feelings about marriage as an institution. There is no point getting into that debate right now. I could manage the pretend relationship with Amy . . . but that is as far as I will venture into the idea of a monogamous commitment. There is no point raising false hopes to Mum or anyone otherwise.
(Turns to Oyin) Oyin is the better candidate.

Silence

Oyin *(After a moment)* Ok fine, I'll do it.

Kike *(Appears shocked)* You will?

Oyin I will need to think it through properly, but yes . . . yes, okay!

Yomi Good! We don't have a lot of time. Kike, you can pack a few things; I have a friend who lives close by. Amy can drop you off. Stay for a few days and she'll come pick you up after Mum leaves.

Kike I am not staying with any of your friends!

Amy Kike can stay at my place. I am happy to accommodate her for a few days.

Kike Thank you Amy, please help me up.

Amy assists Kike and the two go off together into the bedroom, leaving a moment of strained silence between Oyin and Yomi.

Oyin Yomi, what exactly are we doing?

Yomi I need some time to think clearly but I will sort this all out; I promise.

Oyin *(Brief pause)* The girl in the pictures . . . Why were you kissing her feet?

Pause

Yomi *(Grudgingly)* I don't want to talk about it.

Oyin I need to know. I need to know how bad this is going to get, and what lies ahead.

Yomi is briefly quiet.

Yomi *(Grudgingly)* Only God knows what lies ahead in the affairs of men. We will talk later. Let's get through these next few days in one piece. God help us all.

SCENE ENDS.

SCENE THREE: LEMONS

Mrs O (Mum) walks briskly down the stairs into the living room. She is followed behind by Yomi and Oyin who appear to have been hurrying to catch up with her.

Mrs O Where is Kikelomo?

Yomi and Oyin briefly look to each other before Yomi responds quickly and unconvincingly.

Yomi School. She said she had to return to the campus for coursework.

Mrs O *(With a tinge of impatience)* She told me she will be here this weekend.

Oyin She did? Did Kike know you were coming to Lagos?

Mrs O *(Dismissively)* Never mind. It is unacceptable that I have not set my eyes on that girl since you all left Port Harcourt after the funeral. She hardly calls to speak to her mother — except when there is a problem. Call Kike. Tell her I want her here this weekend. I want everyone here, to honour your father's remembrance — together as a family. That is what he would have wanted.

Yomi *(Mumbles)* Honestly Mum, I would prefer to get through the next few days in quietness by myself.

Mrs O Don't be silly! We all have our obligations to this family — you should know that. When your sister gets here, I need to speak to all three of you. This family has groped in the darkness of grief over the past year. It is time for us to step into the light and demonstrate the beacon of hope your father established this family to be. There are three things your father stood for and built this family and the church on — *(Briefly turns to Yomi)* Faith, integrity, and love. We will continue to stand unwaveringly on those ideals. That is your father's legacy.

Yomi *(Dry laugh)* It almost sounds like a directed admonition.

Mrs O I am only reminding you. You are, after all, the only son of your father and the one to step into his shoes as Archbishop someday. Hopefully, I am preaching to the converted. The elders have approved your ordination into a Diocese leadership role. I need a resolution from each one of you, to play your part and to move forward. We all need to pick ourselves up and press on.

Yomi What if we are not ready . . . to move on?

Mrs O *(Briskly whilst rummaging her bag till she pulls out a phone which she dials into whilst speaking)* We cannot grieve forever. Life must go on. Why isn't Kike picking my call?

Yomi *(Interjects, clearly to divert the conversation)* Ah, Oyin has some big news to share!

Oyin Well, it's not big news as such. Let's not get overdramatic.

Yomi You don't need to be modest. A wedding is a big deal. Don't downplay your excitement!

Mrs O Wedding? Whose wedding?

Yomi Oyin is engaged. Stephen proposed to her yesterday.

Mrs O Really? Nobody mentioned that to me.

Oyin *(Struggling with words)* Yes, well . . . we only just discussed this last night. It all happened very quickly. I am honestly still trying to reconcile the whole idea in my head.

Mrs O Stephen did not think it appropriate to ask for my approval before asking you to marry him?

Oyin appears to be baulking, Yomi steps forward quickly with a glass of water.

Yomi *(Attempts to interrupt)* Do you want a drink, Mother? I have some water.

Mrs O *(Pushing the glass aside impatiently)* No, I don't need water! I'm not here for water!

There is a moment of strained silence after which Mrs O lets out a short grunt of disapproval.

Yomi We thought you'd be more *excited* at Oyin's announcement. I mean, you've been saying that you're ready for baby diapers and grandmother duties.

Mrs O Don't patronise me, Yomi; we both know which one of you I'm expecting wedding bells from. There are hundreds of good women at the Church, who would make a suitable wife for you . . . to build a solid Christian home together. *(Impatiently)* I am tired of all your delays and excuses. I mean your father was praying to hold a grandchild before he. . .

Yomi *(Appearing to get agitated)* Mummy, don't start, please!

Mrs O *(Abrupt change in temperament)* I have not even started with you yet! Your father would be turning in his grave!

Oyin Can we please allow Daddy to rest in peace?

Yomi Besides, I'm sure Daddy will have been ecstatic to hear that Oyin and Stephen have scheduled a date for the traditional wedding in two weeks' time.

Oyin turns wide eyes to him.

Mrs O *(She turns unbelieving, questioning eyes to Oyin)* What do you mean, two weeks' time?

Oyin *(With a weak smile)* Well . . . we haven't entirely . . . concluded on a date; we're hoping to get approvals from both parents first.

Yomi *(Continuing for her)* Yes, but since Stephen is scheduled to travel and relocate soon, you both know you really don't have much time to spare. You need things moving quickly, don't you?

Mrs O *(In a reel)* Relocate? What is this about?

Yomi Oyin, haven't you told Mum? We agreed to keep Mum properly *engaged* with this plan, remember?

Mrs O *(With clear disapproval)* No, she hasn't told me any such thing!
(Turning to Oyin) Have you?

Oyin *(Struggling to keep up whilst throwing quick angry glares to Yomi)* It's just that the whole thing has been such a rush; we're still trying to *digest* it ourselves . . .

Yomi Are you sure you don't want some water, Mum?

Mrs O *(With a snap)* No, I do not want water! *(Returning to Oyin)* Well?

Oyin *(Slowly at first but picking up)*
Well . . . Stephen got . . . a promotion and . . . he is being . . . relocated to head office in Zambia. He has just about two weeks to take up the position.

Mrs O We can't have a traditional wedding in two weeks; that is out of the question. You all are clearly out of your minds! Do you think people just wake up and decide that they're going to get married . . . in two weeks! *(Tosses the phone aside in frustration)* Get me your sister on the phone now!

Oyin *(With sudden resolute)* This has nothing to do with Kike. Stephen and I have been together for seven years, Mum. We have always been very clear that we are dating with intentionality. If we decide to get married, that should not take anyone by surprise!

Mrs O Yes, but nobody ever said anything about getting married *tomorrow*. Do you know how much trouble goes into organising a wedding? *(Appearing to be taking a mental stock)* The hall, food, the caterers, aso-ebi . . . we haven't even . . . *(Shaking her head quickly)* It is not possible. Besides, you can't just make decisions and enforce them on us! You younger ones and all your rubbish, modernised ideas; we don't do things that way!
(Turns and addresses Yomi) The cultural rite of passage is that you must give us due notice, after which the family elders will make enquiries and help you decide if this person is right for you or not.

Oyin Right for me? You have known Stephen and his family for many years!

Mrs O Irrespective — these things must go through the normal process. Oyin, you should know better than this. I expect more from you than this haphazard development.

Yomi I think you need to explain the situation surrounding the decision to Mum. You know, how you said that Stephen's relocation right now is indefinite; he doesn't know when next he'll be coming home so he asked you to move to Zambia with him.

Oyin *(She briefly eyes Yomi then continues weakly)* Yes . . . yes, thank you *Pastor* Yomi! We figured we should have the wedding here with our families before we leave.

Mrs O *(Angry outburst)* Leave! You want to just pack up and leave your family — with a ridiculous two weeks' notice! What about your duties at the Church? *(Shaking her head firmly)* It's a good thing I came; you're not rushing anywhere. If Stephen cares for you, he'll wait. If he cannot wait to do things properly, then let him go to Zanzibar . . . or Zimbabwe, there will be other good men.

Oyin *(Splutters with indignation)* You can't decide for me when I will get married! I'm not a child!

Brief pause during which Mrs O sizes her up.

Mrs O *(Calmly)* Where is your ring?

Oyin *(Briefly clueless)* What ring?

Mrs O Your engagement ring.

Brief awkward pause and Oyin turns to Yomi for help.

Yomi It was too tight; Stephen took it away for resizing, didn't he?

Oyin Oh yes. He will return a refitted one tomorrow.

Mrs O *(With a gasp)* Oh my God, these children will be the death of me.

Mrs O suddenly lets out a series of quickened gasps; she begins fanning her face with her hand furiously as a result.

Oyin *(With concern)* Mum, are you okay?

Mrs O *(Amidst gasps)* My medicine . . . get me my anxiety prescriptions quickly! They are in my bag, in the room.

Oyin rushes out of the room. Mrs O watches her leave out of the corner of her eye, then she moves quickly as soon as Oyin is out of sight to grab hold of Yomi's hand.

Mrs O *(Speaking through gritted teeth)* Do I look like a fool to you?

Yomi *(His eyes widening)* Uh?

Mrs O *(Expression suddenly turning furious)* Do you think it would cost me anything to slap the devil out of you right now?

Yomi *(Appears confused)* What . . . what . . . are you talking about?

Mrs O takes in a deep breath in an apparent effort to contain herself.

Mrs O *(With a piercing gaze)* Everything in this family will be done in the right order. You are my first child and your father's only son. You will give me my first grandchild in the proper way, and dutifully take up your responsibilities at the Church. Do you understand me?

Oyin rushes in at the exact moment — in time to see her mother's actual healthy state. She sets the medicine packet in her hand down on the table with a slam that startles her mother.

Oyin Your medicine, Mother!

Mrs O *(Resuming her gasping)* Thank you, Oyin.

Mum moves slowly to collect the packet.

Oyin *(Tersely)* Cut the drama, Mum. I'm not ten years old anymore.

Mrs O rights herself slowly with a momentary guilty flush on her face.

Oyin *(Seriously)* I've made my decision; I'm getting married to Stephen.

Mrs O *(Putting a foot forward and crossing her arms)* I'm not giving you my blessing.

Yomi and Oyin *(In unison)* Uh?

Mrs O You've made your decision; I've made mine too. You can't get married before your brother.

Oyin *(With sincere alarm)* I can't wait for Yomi; he has no intentions of getting married ever!

Mrs O *(Reproaching)* Don't talk about your brother that way! Yomi is a Pastor, with a responsibility to show the congregation the right way of living. *(With finality as she keeps a lethal gaze on Yomi)* Yomi *will* get married and only after he does, can you also. It's obvious there is a need for parental supervision in this house. I need to see urgent changes around here! Otherwise, I will need to extend my visit to one month instead of two weeks originally planned.

Yomi One month! *(Stuttering)* You . . . you can't do that!

Mrs O *(With a mix of perplexity and outrage)* Why not? *Pastor* Yomi, tell me — why not?

Oyin suddenly laughs out loud.

Oyin Of course you can stay a month, Mummy! You should! That will give you adequate time to meet and get to know Yomi's girlfriend. Maybe you can convince him to get married *before Jesus returns.*

There's a moment of silenced pause: Mrs O's face lights up with visible hope.

Mrs O Ah, there is someone, Yoml?

Yomi appears displeased.

Oyin You haven't told Mummy? Have you forgotten that we discussed this too? Her name is Amy; she's a lovely girl! Isn't she, brother?

Mrs O *(Turning slowly to Yomi with an expression of hopeful expectation)* Amy? Really? Is that true, dear?

Yomi *(Ruefully)* Yes, yes, Amy is lovely. She is very helpful.

Mrs O slowly lifts her head and then hands upwards in a gesture of religious appreciation.

Mrs O Wow . . . that's amazing news! *(With a short laugh)* So you like this girl, Amy? I had almost given up hope on you. Your poor mother was starting to worry something was wrong somewhere.
(Turning merrily to Oyin, then audience)
But there is nothing wrong! You have just been praying and waiting for the right woman all along! *(Suddenly moving to grab Yomi excitedly)* God has answered that prayer!

Yomi *(Ruefully)* Yes, yes, it seems He has.

Mrs O *(Unabashed)* Of course, He has! Look at you — you're blushing like a teenager!

Oyin Well, it would have been nice to see this level of excitement at my news also.

Mrs O Don't be silly, Oyin. *This* calls for celebration.

Yomi No celebration, Mum. I think we have all had enough excitement for today. I am going in to get some rest.

Oyin *(Dropping weakly into a chair)* Same here.

Mrs O *(With sudden firmness, through menacing teeth)* I said, this calls for celebration! We will celebrate! You will both invite Stephen and Amy here today. We will thank God, raise a glass, make a toast, and make plans.

Yomi No . . . we can't . . .

Mrs O Why not?

Yomi I am leading the Friday evening service today. I have lots of preparations and Church administrative work to complete.

Mrs O *(Firmly)* No excuses! We will gather here today, all of us. Let your respective partners know. And call your sister Kike; she must be here too. Tell her I want her home — tonight!

She exits briskly, leaving the two to turn gaping expressions to each other.

Yomi What just happened here?

Oyin *(With annoyance)* What do you think? Our Mother just happened!

Oyin marches out, leaving Yomi on stage till blackout.

SCENE ENDS.

I hope to be found by You, like lost sheep and one kobo coin.

SCENE FOUR: LOOSE ENDS

Yomi enters the living room. He is dressed in some form of formal religious attire and holds a Bible. He is deep in thought for a moment before he makes a show of composing himself to deliver a monologue.

Yomi Many of you will know that this weekend marks one year since we said good night to my father, our Archbishop. I want to speak to you today about the complex duality of faith in the face of loss.

This is the word of God, written for the redemption of a broken humanity.

What would it take to believe that this book is true? Faith, hope, wonder . . . simple things. But what will it take, to believe that all of this is a lie?

I once met a man who lost his faith in the parking lot of a hospital. He was kneeling despairingly to the ground, screaming madly to the heavens. A broken man who had just lost a loved one.

I could sense that something had deeply shattered inside him, so, I knelt next to this total stranger, and I cried with him. I cried for him.

After what seemed like an eternity, I picked him up and began what would turn out to be a long walk together — as a pastor and a friend — with a simple earnest desire to heal his deeply wounded heart.

We found a nearby Buka, and I ordered food for him. He did not eat. Instead, we sat in silence, and allowed the night to idle away until the canteen closed shop and the kitchen steward girls exchanged cutleries for stilettos and bouncy skirts.

Grief is a painfully complex road. It will force you to journey far away from the simplicity of delicate faith into strange places. A curious dichotomy of losing ourselves in the hope of being truly, deeply found.

I hope to be found by You, like lost sheep and one kobo coin.

After that fateful day, I met with that man many times to encourage and pray with him. He is drifting away but he never speaks openly about his loss.

Mrs O enters behind him, but he does not notice her. She remains in the background and quietly listens.

Yomi Instead, he would silently curse the heavens and tell me stories of reckless abandon amidst the distant echo of a praying mother urging her son to call on a Saviour who had left an unyielding bitter taste in his mouth.

You see, every time we shut out the light — because life forces us to lose faith in simple things like prayer, hope, and a God of justice — darkness slowly creeps in, and our vices gladly wait to embrace our emptiness. We become wild men with little left to lose, daring to demand answers from the heavens for its negligence.

Pause
There are many broken amongst us. Many who held space and dutifully waited for a promised Messiah — a Saviour who never showed up, even after we desperately begged for His redemption.

My message for the broken among us today is . . .

He pauses and turns his face sadly away from the stage.

My message for the broken today is . . .

Mrs O Are you preparing for your sermon today?

Yomi Mum! I didn't realise you were there.
Yes . . . yes, I am.

She moves to stand behind him and speaks gently.

Mrs O *(Helps him to gently lift his head)* You need to lift your head, raise your voice, and speak with authority and conviction. Tell me, what is your message to the broken?

He remains silent then turns briefly to her.

Yomi Not to give up, even in this place of brokenness.

She holds his gaze quietly for a moment before responding.

Mrs O You know . . . when your father's health started failing last year . . . One day, we both sat alone on the steps of the front porch at home, looking outside into a dark, starless night, wondering what will be.

For the first time in all my years, your father turned to me with defeat in his eyes, and he said to me, "I am tired; my soul is worn out."

I didn't offer any response. Instead, I gently pulled him close, made him sit within my thighs, and proceeded quietly to plait his untidy Afro into fine

Bantu knots. A quiet eternal moment, no words said or needed.

She pauses with apparent introspection.

Mrs O Tell your friends and your congregation that pain is inevitable, for all of us. It will come, again and again and again . . . with the sole intention of breaking us. The question though is, when you are broken and in the process of being ripped to shreds, what virtue will flow out of your desperation?

I need you to always remember who you are, Yomi. You are the son of your father. Nothing . . . nothing in this world could ever change that.

She turns and marches out of the room, pausing briefly near the exit.

Mrs O I listened to all of it. It's a lovely poem but change the message — it is not biblically correct and some of your statements have doctrinal flaws. *(Adds briskly)* Change all of it.

I need to get some rest. Wake me up when Kikelomo and your partners arrive.

She exits and he watches her leave.

Yomi *(Quietly)* My message for the broken is . . .to hold on, till we are found again, like lost sheep and one kobo coin.

He pauses, turns his face away then walks quietly out.

SCENE ENDS.

SCENE FIVE: BEAUTIFUL BLUE DANUBE

Oyin enters the living room and walks to a corner near the edge of the stage, making effort not to be seen or heard. She quickly dials into a phone and begins a hushed urgent conversation.

Oyin *(Desperately)* I'm only asking you to *pretend* that we are getting married . . . What do you mean you're not going to do it?

Pause

Yes, I know it's a lie; I know that! But. . . for all intents and purposes, *we are* going to get married at some point so it's not completely a blatant lie. *(Adds ridiculously)* Think of it like a rehearsal performance.

Pause

Don't . . . Please don't preach to me, Stephen! I am fully aware how ridiculous the idea sounds. I wouldn't be asking for your help if the situation wasn't so stupidly desperate!

Pause

No, she still does not know . . . She doesn't know anything! There are other developments, but I don't have a lot of time to explain right now.

Pause

Why am I getting involved? Because they are my siblings, and I can't just abandon them! Besides, someone with some common sense needs to be able to put an end to everything — that is why I am getting involved.

Pause

Yes, today! She wants to see you this evening.

Pause

All I am asking is that you please get a ring — I need an engagement ring, a believable one. Just go along with the narrative; that is all I am asking.

Pause

No? What do you mean, no? You can't just leave me hanging!

Pause

Stephen!

Pause

Stephen!! Stephen!!!

She pulls the phone away from her ear and stares into it with disbelief.

Oyin He hung up!

Yomi enters quickly. Similarly, he is frantically busy on a mobile phone.

Oyin He hung up! He's not going to do it. I mean, of course he's not going to do it! Anybody with common sense will say the exact the same thing! Yomi, we need to clear this up now. We need to bring Mum in and tell her everything.

Yomi Keep your voice down! You'll wake Mum! We can't tell her anything. We can't stop now!

Oyin Did you not hear what I said? Stephen says he will not be involved at all!

Yomi You must convince him; You're his girlfriend – he'll listen to you. Listen, the situation with the pictures is getting pretty bad. I received a message . . . They sent another picture.

Oyin What do you mean? Why is there another picture?

Yomi That is not the issue right now. They are asking for money — ten million naira! Ten million and they will make the pictures go away forever.

Oyin Ten million naira! Where will you get ten million naira from? We don't have that kind of money just lying around!

Yomi From the church. You need to convince Mum tonight to loan you the money. She can borrow it from the church. Tell her you need a deposit for the wedding — for the event hall and other payments. Do you see what I mean? We need to continue with the plan!

Oyin You want me to lie to Mummy, to steal money from the church? Have you gone mad?!

Yomi Do you have a better idea? I need the money before tomorrow; otherwise, they are threatening to upload the photos all over social media.

Oyin How about if you tell the truth. The truth doesn't cost ten million naira! Let the pictures come out, then convince Kike to tell Mum about the baby. The truth will set us all free from this madness!

Yomi *(With harsh cynicism)* The truth isn't going to fix this. The truth will have me removed from the church leadership and tarnish our family's image.

Oyin If you are so convinced, then do it yourself! Ask Mum for the loan yourself. Don't involve me in your deception *and depravity.*

Yomi *(Through gritted teeth)* Everybody has a duty to perform here. The situation is what it is, and you know what consequences are at stake for this family. You can choose not to play your part but rest assured that your passivity will have contributed to Daddy's legacy being ripped to shreds by this scandal. There is no trust fund waiting for anyone to pick our lives up after you burn the whole thing to the ground whilst you are trying to take the moral high ground.

Oyin I don't care! I don't care about all your lies and deception! I have no hand in all of this! Call the girls you were messing around with and ask them to start a go-fund-me petition on your behalf! Listen to yourself, *Pastor* Yomi. You are a few days away from your ordination and there is no clarity at all about what exactly you stand for or believe in! Tell the truth; otherwise, I will do it for you and for Kike too!

If this leads to the end of your ministry, maybe I will have done the right thing in God's eyes and, just maybe, you will find redemption from the ashes of your ruins!

Yomi We are all depraved one way or the other. You are not God — you can't judge me because of my mistakes.

Oyin Mistakes? Something has changed in you, deeply changed since Daddy died.

Yomi What do you mean? Something changed *for* everyone. It is called grief — the pain of deep loss.

Oyin That is not what I am talking about Yomi. When I look into your eyes, I see something deeper than grief. The person being unveiled to me today over the past four hours feels like a total stranger. When I look into your eyes, I see . . . I see a caged wild man, and it scares me. What happened to my brother? Who are you exactly?

Pause

Yomi *(Quietly)* You can't deal with the truth, Oyin.

Oyin Don't patronise me, Yomi. *(Continues after a brief pause)*
Do you remember Daddy used to say, "*How can you be the person God has called you to be, when you cannot be honest with yourself about who you really are in the first place?*" The problem with living a lie is that when the fences finally fall, the whole street will see your nakedness.

Yomi *(Short dry laugh)* What if I told you, and everyone who cares to know, what the truth is. Ever since Daddy left us, I am no longer sure what I believe in anymore. My devotion is tainted, with little left, except unattended resentment and this urgent anxiety to fully live and embrace life before my own time is spent.

What if I told you the truth is, I have given up waiting for a God who never showed up and whose face I cannot see. So instead, I am looking for simple pleasures — the type that will not damn my soul with unmet expectations. What if I told you the truth is, I have found an easier path that is intricately beautiful in its own complexity. A depth that knows how to warm your soul like nothing else can.

What is truth? It is a curious irony finding yourself amid losing yourself.

Oyin slowly lowers herself to sit, appearing as a mixture of shock, sadness, and disappointment.

Oyin *(With a painful whisper)* You are rejecting God because Daddy died? Everybody dies — that is the whole essence of the gospel.

Yomi It's not just that he died! It's why he died; how he died! God's general, they called him! Yet, God was either too busy or incompetent to deliver His own from cancer!

Oyin Don't speak like that! You can't speak like that — you are *the Pastor*! Listen to yourself! Everything you have said today is a walking contradiction.

Long Pause

You can't accept the ordination, Yomi! You can't even get your own life together, much less lead the Church.

Yomi You think I don't know that? It may be hard for you to fathom it, but maybe there is honour within confusion and depravity. If you are so sure of own your convictions, please be my guest and tell our mother, the church, and everyone who cares to know that Daddy, the most revered Archbishop, saw his dying visions wrong. Tell them his son is not the person God told him I am, and so someone else must accept the ordination. Please tell them; be my guest!

Tense silence.

Amy enters. She notices the tense situation in the room and pauses momentarily.

Amy Pastor Yomi asked me to return here after dropping Kike. You said your mother wanted to meet me.

Tempers are intentionally calmed, and the ensuing conversation is calmer and softer toned.

Oyin Yes . . . Is she okay? I mean Kike.

Amy Yes. Yes, she is. She is settling well. Has your mother arrived?

Yomi Yes. She's taking a nap. I'll go check on her. She is keen to meet you.

Yomi starts to make his way out until Amy stops him.

Amy What do you want me to say to her — about us?

Yomi *(Dismissively)* Anything will do. Nothing sensational. The real focus should be on Oyin and Stephen's wedding, like we all agreed.

He exits.

Amy How is she — your Mum?

Oyin Same as always. She has a lot going on, so she may come across confrontational. Brace yourself.

Amy *(Appears hesitant)* Oyin, can I speak to you, privately?

Oyin Yes . . . yes, sure.
(Looks about cautiously) Yomi told me they are asking for money — for the photos.

Amy Yes . . . It's not about that though . . . It's just that . . . I don't think I can follow through, with . . . all of this . . .

Oyin Of course . . . It's not an ideal situation for your pastor to ask you to tell lies on his behalf — in your first week on the job. It is no doubt a ridiculous first impression, but I promise you this is not what our family or the Church stands for.

Amy I know. It's not just about the lies and pretence. *(Brief pause)* Kike says she is quite close to you.

Oyin *(Fondly)* Yes . . . we used to be until . . . until Dad and everything else that has happened afterwards.

Amy Are you speaking with her?

Oyin I try, but she's completely closed off. The thing is . . . Kike was always Daddy's baby girl. She took his passing quite tough. Somewhere in between struggling to deal with loss, grief, and trying to make sense of a very public faith that no longer seems to reconcile, the baby happened. I have tried but she won't tell me anything except that she is determined not to keep the child.

Amy *(Gently)* She is carrying a lot — I mean, you all are. Grief is tough for anyone, but the rest of you are adults. Kike is just a child . . .

Oyin Has she told you anything?

Amy *(After a brief hesitation)* Whatever she decides to do with the baby is only half the problem. She is going to need a lot of help to get through all that she has going on.

Mrs O enters with Yomi following behind her.

Mrs O *(With a gentle smile)* You must be Amy.

Amy Yes, Ma.

Amy moves close to her and kneels to greet her with sombre respect.

Mrs O It is good to finally meet you.

Mrs O helps her stand and takes her into a warm prolonged embrace until she releases her with a knowing smile at Yomi.

Mrs O She is the one. I can feel it in my spirit — the one you have waited so long for!

Yomi *(Dry laugh)* I am glad to see such a warm connection. I imagine there is a lot of *getting-to-know-you* to be done, but Oyin has some important wedding developments we were waiting to discuss with you, Mum.

Mrs O *(Dismissively)* I'm certain Oyin's discussion can wait. I want to know everything about this lovely woman who has stolen my son's heart. We have so much to talk about, in so little time. Tell me, Amy, how did you know that he is the one?

Amy appears to think for a moment.

Amy *(Speaks with eyes intently fixed on Yomi)* He has an uncommon way with words. I attended the church six months ago and heard him speak. His words make you feel like you are the only person in the room, like you have known each other since the beginning of eternity. I fell in love with his words.

Mrs O· *(Laughs heartily)* Yes, his tongue is like the hand of a skilled writer — just like his father. My husband used to say, "Beware of the cunning linguist Man of God." I didn't understand his pun until many years later. But he has a good heart, my Yomi does.

Amy *(Laughs out loud)* I remember the specific sermon. I bought the recording, and I must have listened to it a hundred times. It was called 'Watershed at the Beautiful Blue Danube.'
(Turns to Yomi)
Do you remember it, Pastor? You told a story about a man who was battling a deconstruction of his faith. You said it was a retelling of the story of the Prodigal Son. You started the sermon with a short parable — do you remember?

Yomi Yes, I remember that teaching.
(Muses thoughtfully)
Last night, we dipped our feet into the beautiful blue Danube, and watched a magnificent Cathedral slowly implode into rubble.
They said she had survived many wars and disasters, but something dangerously subtle had been occurring within her walls. I remember that teaching very clearly. I didn't realise you were in the congregation that day.

Amy That teaching helped me through a difficult season of my faith — a dark night of the soul. You should listen to it again. It felt like everything you said was directly from the mouth of God.

Yomi Yes . . . I'm sure it was.

Mrs O Oh, look at that, just look at that! It's a beautiful love story right in front of our eyes! Your father would have been so blessed to see this day! We must sit down to a meal — everyone! Yomi, I brought some pepper soup mix. They're in the kitchen. Can you go with Amy to show her how to heat some up for me?

Amy Yes certainly, Ma.

Mrs O Don't be silly — you can call me Mum.

Yomi appears speechless for a moment, then he turns and storms out of the room. Amy follows slowly behind him.
Oyin moves to follow her, but Mrs O stops her.

Mrs O *(Beckoning her over)* Come and sit with me for a moment, Oyin; I need to speak with you.

Oyin returns to her side with slow steps and a suspicious expression on her face.

Mrs O *(Checking briefly for Yomi's absence, she turns to her with a piercing gaze and a dead serious expression)* Oyin, I might be getting old but I'm sure you know that I am not foolish.

Oyin *(Slowly)* Yes, Mummy.

Mrs O I still have very keen senses. In fact, I can put one and two together before most people can even tell that there are numbers on the table.

Oyin *(Looking back apprehensively for Yomi's return)* Yes, yes . . . we know that. You used to say that mother always knows everything?

Mrs O I am not God, but that is true too.

(Pauses for a moment) I've been doing a lot of thinking since I arrived.

Oyin Oh . . .

Mrs O Mother's intuition or whatever, but I can tell that something's not quite right; don't you agree?

Oyin What . . . what do you mean, Mum?

Mrs O *(Leans forward to squint at her)* I raised you all to give precedence to certain important values such as integrity, honesty, order . . . things don't appear to be in order. I have been praying to God about it . . .

Oyin *(Quickly with panic)* Oh, God, Mum. I can explain!

Mrs O *(Calmly)* Shh, don't get ahead of yourself, dear.

Oyin *(Continues in a frenzy)* I did say that we should speak with you all along but . . .

Mrs O *(Cutting her off)* I don't have a problem with your intentions, Oyin — it's how you have decided to go about things. I know that Yomi and Kike can be entirely unreliable, but I honestly expected much more from you.

Oyin I know, Mum. I tried to talk her out of it but . . .

Mrs O *(Watches her quietly for a second)* It is not the time for blame games. We need to move on and do things right — we always need to do things right. That is why I have considered these things out clearly and . . . I have decided that . . .

She appears to think for a moment; Oyin awaits her finish with apparent dread.

Mrs O . . . you and Stephen can get married like you've planned.

Oyin *(With a gasp and appearing taken aback for a moment)* Uh?!

Mrs O I will overlook the irresponsible way you have both chosen to go about things and I will give my blessings to your plans — on behalf of your father and I.

Oyin *(With disbelief)* You will?

Mrs O *(Continuing in a torrent)* Yes, I will. Although these two weeks madness remains highly unreasonable! We will need at least two months to get ready and do things properly. We will do things properly.

Oyin appears horrified.

Mrs O We'll start making the phone calls immediately — to let the families understand the circumstances surrounding the rush; we'll do a lot of invitations by mouth before the prints are out.

Oyin *(With a stutter)* But . . . but . . .

Mrs O Don't stutter, dear; it's not feminine.

Oyin *(Quickly)* Yes, Mum. But . . . I've also been doing some thinking myself and I think that your reasoning was right. There really is no rush . . . I mean, a lifetime is a long time to make such a decision in a short time. There is no rush, really — Stephen and I can wait.

Mrs O *(With a wave of the hand)* Nonsense; don't let your old woman kill your enthusiasm. Where else do you think you'll find a perfect gentleman like Stephen?

Oyin *(Desperately)* Stephen is not like that; he'll wait. We'll both wait for each other.

Mrs O *(With imposing finality)* I have made my decision! I will give my blessing and you two will get married in two months!

Oyin But . . . but . . . Stephen will completely freak out!

Mrs O Don't you worry, honey; you'll make a beautiful bride.
(Brief Pause) But there is one small consideration, in return for my flexibility.

Oyin *(With a suspicious yet hopeful expression)* What's that?

Mrs O *(Confirms Yomi's absence)* I need your help with your brother. Amy is a good girl . . . I need you to help me make it work — for the two of them.
I need your brother to settle down, put his house in order, and start to build a home together with Amy.

Oyin Yomi, settle down with Amy. Do you mean, get married? That is never going to happen!
(With an incredulous laugh and mutters under her breath)
There is no *Shakespearean Taming of the Shrew* going to happen here, except by a miracle.

Mrs O *(Firmly)* Keep your voice down. If I wanted Yomi to be part of this discussion, I would have invited him. Do you know how long I have worried about him? He will be forty next year, and the church elders are raising eyebrows already. An elder must be above reproach, the husband of one wife, temperate, uncontentious, a good manager of his household, one who has his children. Those are Biblical principles which the church subscribes wholly to. The exception to your father's wishes can only last for so long. Yomi must take a wife, and Amy is a good woman.

Oyin But you have only just met her today! You don't know anything about her, and frankly neither does Yomi!

Mrs O I don't think that is any of your business.

Oyin *(Spluttering)* But, that's insane!

Mrs O *(Firmly)* Watch your tongue!
(Gets up) That is my final word; I'll give you time to think about it. I will give my consent to your wedding plans, but only after Amy is also wearing an engagement ring — from your brother.

Oyin You can't impose that on me! And . . . and even if you want to . . . I'm not ready to get married anyway!

Mrs O *(With a smile as she leaves)* Oh but you are dear; you forget you're already engaged. I think that puts us all in a very *fitting* position. All you need to do is put in a few words and some nudging encouragement for your brother every now and then. You are the sensible one — everyone listens to you. I have been praying about this and I need you to work with me.

Oyin makes another protest but Mrs O cuts her off.

Mrs O I'll go check up on the two love birds.

(Motions briefly at her fingers) You need to sort out that engagement ring.

She exits.

SCENE ENDS.

SCENE SIX: CHARIOT

Yomi is alone on stage, holding a phone. He appears to be expecting a call and shows visible signs of anxiety. The phone finally rings. He hurries to the edge of the stage to answer the call. The ensuing monologue reflects a one-sided version of his discussion on the phone. All the while, he makes a visible effort to contain his anger and frustration.

Yomi I am working on it. It is a lot of money; I need some more time! Give me some more time and I will get it to you.

Pause
But I need evidence that the pictures will be permanently destroyed.

Pause

I am not messing around. I know that the photos are damaging; I have seen them. Those pictures will ruin everything — my family, the church, people's lives, and faith.

Pause
Three hours is not enough time. Give me till tomorrow, please.

Pause

Listen, I am a pastor, a man of God, a man . . . *(He adds defeatedly)* I am begging . . . I am begging you — please!

Pause

He pulls the phone away as it appears the call has abruptly ended. He takes a momentary pause, then speaks slowly and thoughtfully in monologue.

I once met a girl, with the beauty of the gods. Carefree and untamed like fireflies. Wild like majestic cascading waterfalls. She spoke with the alluring decibel of an angel. Talia, like the Dew of Heavens. If only I had known that the little demon was out to ruin my life.

Mrs O enters. She drags along a large bag visibly filled with clothes.

Mrs O Was that Kikelomo on the phone?

Yomi No. No, it wasn't. Mum, I need to speak with you.

She pauses to consider him briefly before responding.

Mrs O Your father used to say that there is a time for everything, and everything has its own time. I promised myself that this weekend I will remember him well. Without tears, without the painful memories of sickness or sadness. I want to remember well, with a heart full of love and thankfulness. That is all I want to do. There is a time to speak and a time to be silent. Now is the time for silence; we will talk later. Do you understand, Yomi?

Yomi Yes. Yes, Mum.

Mrs O sits, rummages in the bag and pulls out some clothes one by one.

Mrs O I dug around in your wardrobes to find something suitable.

Yomi Suitable for what? Those are the clothes we wore for Dad's funeral last year.

Mrs O I Know that. I wasn't planning to come here for an impromptu wedding, so anything decent will do.

Yomi *(Appalled)* We can't wear funeral clothes for a wedding.

Mrs O *(Sharply)* Don't be dramatic. We all need to be considerate of the situation – for your sister. I've made some emergency calls to get things going. You will all return with me to Port Harcourt. We have a very short window to meet the extended families and start discussions for the engagement ceremonies. Try this on; It looked good on you last year.

Yomi I am never wearing those clothes — ever again! They remind me of death.

She appears to ignore his tirade.

Mrs O It may be tricky to get the whole family together at such short notice but I'm sure a large number will turn out for the cause. Don't you think so? Oyinlola is the darling of our family.

Oyin and Amy enter; Mrs O doesn't notice them initially.

Oyin *(Stepping slowly into the room)* Oh-my-God . . . What are these, Mum?

Mrs O Oyin, I was waiting for you.

Oyin *(With awe)* Mum . . . what . . . are all these?

Mrs O Clothes, Oyin – for the wedding. We will need clothes for the ceremonies, and there isn't really a lot of time to make new ones.

Oyin *(Still in a reel)* I can see they are clothes, but where did you get these from?

Mrs O *(Clearly disconnected and speaking in a rush)* I brought some from Port Harcourt, for this weekend — for your father's memorial dinner. But I was thinking this might be more suited to a wedding. We don't have a lot of time, you know.
(Pulls out a shoe box and opens it)
I need to get your opinion about your preferred colour theme and shoes. What do you think about fuchsia pink? I bought a size eight for you — your shoe size hasn't changed, right?

Oyin *(Taking in the goods with disbelief)* No, Mum . . . I don't think so. But who is paying for all these?

Mrs O moves to pick up a strip of fabric and holds it up to her chest.

Mrs O What do you think of this for Yomi? We could go with a subtle shade of grey and pink. What do you think, Yomi?

Yomi I . . . I don't know.

She picks up another strip of fabric.

Mrs O I got the same design in white too. See, it has tiny yellow sequence all over it. White is pure, like a dove; I think it is classic for engagements — for celebrating instead of . . .
(She drifts off briefly into melancholy)
Instead of mourning.
(Shows it off)

What do you think, Oyin?

Oyin sights a receipt in one of the bags; she pulls it out and lets out a gasp.

Oyin Two hundred and fifty thousand, for *(Skims through the paper)* a pair of shoes!

Mrs O *(Looks around quickly, picks up a pair from the floor and holds them up)* Yes, that's this one. I got that in black. Although I would have preferred anything but black; it seems to match the yellow best.

Oyin *(Stamping a foot with annoyed frustration)* Mum, you're not listening to me!

Mrs O is abruptly quietened, her face mirroring troubled thoughts. She drops the fabric on the chair and looks away.

Oyin *(With immediate concern)* Mum, what's wrong?

She moves to her side; Mrs O remains silent.

Oyin What's the matter? Are you okay? . . . I'm sorry. I'm just trying to take it all in. All this planning, and shopping, and . . .

Mrs O *(Soberly)* Do you think this is easy for me either?

Oyin *(After a moment)* I know, Mum . . . I'm sorry.

Mrs O moves to clear a chair; she sits.

Mrs O Do you think I'm not also losing my mind?

Mrs O bites her lip, swallowing her words; her face glazes with thoughts.

Mrs O Do you know what it takes to raise a child, Oyin? For all those years, nurturing and hoping for the best for her.

Oyin *(Ruefully)* No, but apparently, it'll soon be my turn to discover.

Mrs O We don't ask for much, you know. We don't ask for anything in return for all the years of labour and toil, only that your children will make you proud — not put us to shame. Is that too much to ask?

Oyin *(Kneels by her side)* No it isn't, Mum. It isn't at all. And you know we're not going to do anything short of that. We will make you proud, every single one of us.

Mrs O Things must be done the right way. Do you understand what I am saying — both of you?

Yomi *(Nodding his head in agreement and speaking reassuringly)* Yes, everything will be fine; you need to stop worrying so much.

Mrs O lets out a sigh. Oyin reaches for a strip of fabric and unwinds it.

Oyin *(Lightly, after a surrendering low moan)* You know what, let's forget about how much these things cost for now. They're already here, paid for, so we'll just . . . make the best use of them.
(Places fabric to her chest)
What do you think I should make with this one? A flowing gown maybe?

Mrs O *(Regaining her composure and responding casually)* That one is not for you.

Oyin *(Shortly perplexed)* Oh.
(Reaches for another) This one is nice.

Mrs O That one is not yours either *(Pulls out a penned list)* I started scribbling a dowry request list — you know we need to prepare ahead. The things the man's family must buy and present at the engagement ceremony.
(Reads out)
We will need things like suitcases, food gifts like baskets of fruits, bags of rice, tubers of yam . . .

Oyin *(Appears panicky)* When do we need to buy these, Mum? This is all moving too quickly . . . I don't think I'm ready! I need to discuss this with Stephen also.

Mrs O People usually start getting these items ready weeks before the engagement. We'll need some of them in Port Harcourt when we go and visit the grandparents. We will need to notify them properly — that is the cultural expectation.
(Hands the list to Amy)
You can skim through it; do you think I have missed anything?

Yomi gently snatches the list from Amy's grasp.

Yomi Why are you showing it to her? Oyin is the one getting married here!

He hands the list to Oyin who collects the paper and reads through it with widening eyes.

Mrs O *(With a shrug)* There's nothing wrong with carrying Amy along so she doesn't feel left out.
(Turns a patronising smile to Amy)
Don't worry, you are already part of the family. In fact, you can go for a matching colour with Yomi.

(Pulls out a piece of fabric from the bag and places it across Amy's shoulder)
You must join us for all the ceremonies when we all get to Port Harcourt.

Yomi What do you mean 'we'?

Mrs O *(Cheerfully)* Oh, Amy's coming with us to Port Harcourt. I spoke to your uncle. He suggested that we better all come down sooner than later so that the elders can start the engagement discussions. There are flights to Port Harcourt on Monday.

Yomi Monday!

Oyin *(Throws up hands in frustration)* Can we just slow things down please!

Mrs O Have you forgotten that Stephen has limited time before he travels? We can't move slowly. We will all return to Port Harcourt and work together to make this happen. You should be grateful for my flexibility.

Yomi I can't go to Port Harcourt; I have responsibilities here in Lagos!

Mrs O You also have responsibilities in Port Harcourt; you can't afford not to be there. You have an important role to play, in your father's absence.

Yomi You're not listening to me. I said I'm not going anywhere! And neither is Amy!

Mrs O Yes, you are, dear; and don't raise your voice at your mother! Amy says she'll be happy to come with us.

Yomi *(Whirls furiously to face Amy)* We haven't quite discussed that, have we, *darling?*

Amy *(With cautious hesitation)* No we haven't, but with everything going on, I thought it would be a good idea to get away from . . . everything, you know . . .

Yomi *(Raising his voice)* You are crossing the line!

Mrs O Yomi! Don't speak to her like that!

Yomi I'm not going anywhere, Mum, and neither is Amy!

Mrs O Stop behaving like a child! We all must make sacrifices to make this *wedding work*. Take a break from church duties for a week. I'm sure the Diocese will understand.

Oyin *(Weakly)* It's a very busy period at the office, Mum. My next leave isn't due till next year.

Mrs O *(With a short laugh)* Very funny. So, when exactly do you plan to get married — during lunch break?

Oyin Mum, I think we should discuss this. A trip to Port Harcourt was not part of anybody's plan.

Mrs O *(Getting up and speaking with bitter finality)* Preparing for an emergency wedding was not part of my schedule either! But a problem came up; it had to be dealt with, so I adjusted my plans to fit the situation. You can all do the same. You will all do the same.

She pushes away from the table and walks towards the kitchen.

Mrs O Oyin, come with me. I need to speak with you.

Oyin briefly hesitates, then hurries off behind her, leaving Yomi and Amy alone.

SCENE ENDS.

Carefree and untamed like fireflies.

SCENE SEVEN: GODS OF MEN

***Yomi and Amy are alone in the living room.
There is tense silence to begin.***

Amy I need to speak with you.

Yomi About what?

Amy About Talia. I need to speak to you about Talia.

Yomi *(Pauses to acknowledge)* Who is Talia?

Amy The girl in the pictures.

Yomi *(Gruffly)* I don't know who you are talking about.

Amy *(Looks away with a tinge of embarrassment)* The girl whose feet you were kissing, in the pictures.

Brief pause

Yomi You know, there is a fine line between respecting privacy and doing your job. You are crossing that line.

Amy I am aware. I spoke to her — to Talia. She said a lot of strange things. She said she met you on a website, an alternative lifestyle website. You have had previous interactions with her. She said you both agreed to go to the party together, so you must have known her age.

Yomi I didn't know that she is a teenager!

Amy She called you her slave. Pastor Yomi, she called you her devoted slave.

Yomi I don't know what that means.

Amy She said you are devoted to her. She said you knew about the pictures, and you gave consent to do everything she asks of you – like a slave.

Yomi She wasn't supposed to share the pictures! I didn't give consent to that!

Amy She said . . . she said she owned you and you understand everything that is happening.

Yomi That is rubbish! I certainly did not give consent to anyone blackmailing me!

Brief silence

Amy She called you a pig, Pastor Yomi. Why are you protecting this girl? You should report to the police.

Yomi I don't want to talk about this.

Amy Why?

Yomi *(Dismissively)* It is beyond your level of understanding.

Amy *(With sarcasm)* How? Is it a deeper level of theology or grace that belongs only to Pastors? Are you in love with her?

Yomi *(Rudely)* What is to you? Do I look like the kind of man that falls in love with little girls?

Amy What is it then? Infatuation, obsession, adoration?

Yomi All human beings have an innate desire a need to worship something or someone.

Amy What does that mean? How many girls should we expect to come out with dirty secrets?

Yomi Mind your tone. I am your pastor!

Amy Are you really? Because that is exactly what confuses me. If you were just another man, we wouldn't be having this back and forth, trying to decipher the blurred lines between depravity and your professed authority of faith. You say you are a man of God, a pastor, but are you really?

Yomi You have no idea what it means to be a man of faith, yet still very much a man. It's complicated and I don't expect you to understand.

Amy Lust and every depravity she breeds is not complicated. They are as common as dogs, rabbits, and wild monkeys. Godliness with contentment in this modern world is complicated. You should know that – you are a man of faith, a pastor.

He is quiet.

Amy Kike says you have an alcohol addiction. She said you have also been dabbling with drugs.

Yomi Kike is a misguided child. If I were you, I'd be careful not to take anything she tells you at face value.

Amy The police report said you were under the influence of alcohol and narcotics when you were arrested.

Yomi That is not true!

Amy Are the police also misguided? Kike says . . . She said it wasn't the first time. She said it's not the first time you returned home drunk and completely wasted. People indulge in these things as a means of escape. What are you running from?

Yomi What exactly is this interrogation about? I don't owe you any explanation!

Amy It's my job to protect you, your integrity, and the Church.
(Pause)
I think you need help, Pastor. I think you have problems, and you need professional help.

Yomi *(Casually)* Professional help? Do you think anything is impossible for God?

Amy The problem is, I don't think you believe that yourself.

Yomi You have no idea what you are talking about!

Amy You know, I lost both my parents within a short space of time. I understand your loss, your pain, and the things we do to medicate our trauma. When you lose a parent, what you lose is someone who loves you unconditionally, prays for you immeasurably. Losing a parent is sad; losing two parents is a tragedy – a cultural outrage. It messes you up. I understand your pain; let me help you.

Yomi does not respond for a brief while.

Yomi You don't know anything about me.

Amy Then help me understand. Otherwise, I can't do this. I can't stand with you, stand for you, or represent you, if I don't know what exactly you believe in. Forget the pulpit, the church, and your family. When it comes down to just you and your private, deeply felt convictions, what is the truth? What is your truth?

Yomi What is truth? *(After a brief introspective pause)* Sometimes I think faith is delusional.

Amy A season of doubt is a common response to the trauma of loss.

Yomi I gave a sermon last week about the crucifixion. The text talks about dead people awakening from the grave. Do you believe in zombies?

Amy You are an intelligent man. You should doubt your doubts to the same degree at which you doubt your faith — with logic and common sense. What do you think lies at the end of the path you are treading?

Yomi *(Introspective pause)* I think that there are three important things every man must contend with and reach his own personal convictions – his personal response to the faith of his fathers, the pursuit of his own happiness, and how he will fight the demons that seek to damn him to hell. His conviction across these three things must be solid and unyielding enough to build a life upon. Without a firm conclusion on any of those things, every one of us will falter sooner or later.

Amy And where do you stand?

Yomi I don't know. I think that my ideas of life, love and faith have become deeply flawed – tainted by loss. Every man has two lives. One before he encounters loss and the second which begins after he understands death. Let me ask you a question.

When a storm ravages a land and leaves behind wreckage and disorder, whose fault is the carnage – man or God?

Amy You choose to blame God? It is an easy deflection to blame our depravity as vengeance to the heavens. Did your grief lead you to the whorehouse, to Talia?

He ignores her.

Yomi Can we leave aside all the religious talk and focus on what is important. Listen, I have managed to raise some money.

Amy Where did you get money from?

Yomi I pulled some money from my dad's life insurance payout. I need your help to get the balance.

Amy Your father left specific instructions – that money was to be kept aside for your mother's wellbeing!

Yomi I don't have any other choice, do I?
I need you to speak to Oyin to get the rest of the money from my mother. I am running out of time.

Amy You want your mother to steal money from the church on your behalf?

Yomi Have you got a better idea?

Amy No i don't.

Yomi Exactly. I don't either. At the end of the day, I am a man just like any other man, deeply in need of redemption.

Amy Yet you are a pastor.

Yomi *(He nods with sobriety)* Yet I am a pastor.

He ponders briefly, then exits slowly, leaving her alone on stage till blackout.

SCENE ENDS.

SCENE EIGHT: EVERYTHING

Mrs O enters in with Amy, both dragging in a large suitcase together which they drop mid stage and then stop to talk in hushed tones.

Amy Aren't we going to tell them something? You need to say something today, please.

Mrs O *(Shaking her head)* Not just yet. It is better this way. If we say anything now, everything will fall apart. Stick to the plan.
Pause
Are you worried?

Amy I am scared.

Mrs O *(After a brief pause)* Don't worry; everything will work out. I promise you that things will start to settle soon. Is your suitcase here – all packed up?

Amy It is in the car.

Mrs O Good. *(Adds firmly)* Let's get them inside here.

The two exits, and Yomi enters shortly afterwards.
He sees the suitcases and appears puzzled.

Yomi What is all of this?

He looks around, sees no one then heads purposefully to the luggage and opens it up.

Yomi What is this?
(Visibly shocked at the contents)
What does this woman think she is doing?
(Rummaging through the suitcase and letting off a gasp)

Yomi moves to a second suitcase and opens it quickly. Oyin enters hastily. Yomi turns to Oyin, still amazed.

Yomi *(With exclamation)* These . . . these are all mine!
(Turns with confusion to Oyin)
Did you pack these Oyin? The two suitcases are filled with my things! Why are they filled with my things?

Oyin Why are you asking me? I don't know.

She is cut short by Mrs O and Amy who enter logging in another large suitcase. They dump it in the middle of the room, leaving the three stunned.

Mrs O *(With sudden alarm)* Why are you messing with that suitcase?

She moves quickly to shove Yomi away from the luggage.

Can't you see I've already packed that up?

Yomi *(Obstinately)* Yes, I can see that! All the things you've packed are mine! Why do you have two suitcases filled with my things?

Mrs O I helped you start packing up your belongings.

Oyin What belongings?

Yomi Why? To where?

Mrs O *(Authoritatively)* We can discuss this later. Are you going to just hang around looking at me? Help me with this suitcase!

Oyin helps her to move the suitcase to the centre of the space.

Oyin Mum, what is this? What is going on?

Mrs O There are more suitcases in the bedroom. Come Amy, help me bring them out.

Mrs O marches out, into the bedroom. Amy reluctantly follows her, leaving Yomi and Oyin behind.

Oyin She is not acting like herself! Yomi, I am really confused!

Oyin quickly opens the suitcase and finds some slips of paper. She picks them up and reads the content.

Oyin Flight tickets? Travel tickets to Port Harcourt! *(Thrusting the ticket to Yomi's face)*
Flight bookings for tomorrow morning! *Real* flight booking with *real* departure time!

Yomi Where did she get those from?

Oyin How am I supposed to know? This was all supposed to remain fake, but these are *real* tickets! *(Flicks quickly through the documents)*
She has purchased tickets for all of us to return with her to Port Harcourt!

Yomi Let me see that, and can you please calm down!

Oyin No, I cannot calm down! She has probably been making phone calls to all our family to attend this event! This . . . fake event! Stephen is not even in support of all this madness! Do you expect me to walk down the aisle by myself?

Yomi I said keep your voice down! We just need to play along and keep up the charade, that's all.

Oyin Play along? Have you gone mad?

Yomi *(Reduces tone to a hushed whisper)* We could spin this around and get Mum to return by herself to Port Harcourt on Monday. We could just play along to keep her happy. Neither of us will be boarding that flight.

Oyin (Wildly) You want me to play along and dance my way unwittingly into a non-existent wedding ceremony? I am done with all of this. I'm calling Kike right now to let her know . . .
(Pulls out a phone and begins dialling furiously)
 . . . to let her know that I am done!

She starts to make a phone call.

Yomi Oyin, I need you to think of the reason why we are doing this! This was the plan all along. It is still all under control.

Oyin Control? There is no control! There was never any control in this disaster! We're all on a runaway train that is heading fast towards a wreck! There are no brakes and so I'm jumping off! I've had enough of this . . . fiasco! Kike needs to return here and sort this all out; otherwise, you all leave me no choice but to tell Mum the truth myself – the whole truth!

Mrs O returns with Amy, both carrying smaller suitcases.

Oyin Mum! We need to talk; we need to talk urgently! What are these tickets for?

Mrs O Where did you get those from?
(She moves quickly to grab the tickets)
Give that to me! I'm tired of answering silly questions! You know what, let's just leave right now! We'll go to the airport today! If we hurry, we can catch the evening return flight to Port Harcourt tonight.

Yomi *(With alarm)* Today? We can't leave today! I haven't sent the money! Oyin, you need to speak to Mum about the money! I need to send the rest of the money today.

Mrs O What are you talking about? Amy, please call a taxi. We need a large taxi, for all of us.

Oyin We are not calling any taxi! What about Stephen? I'm not going to get married without Stephen! You haven't even spoken to him in all of this!

Mrs O Help me move these suitcases to the door. *(She moves to pick one up, motioning for Amy to do same)* We haven't got much time.

Oyin moves quickly and jerks the suitcase from her grip.

Mrs O *(Shocked)* Oyin! Have you lost your mind?

Oyin *(Looking wildly to Yomi)* Help me stop her, Yomi! Grab the other suitcases!

Yomi moves to grab a suitcase but Amy rushes forward and takes it away.

Mrs O What is the meaning of this nonsense?

Oyin We have to wait for Kike! We can't travel without Kike!

Mrs O *(Authoritatively)* Kike will be here; she understands the urgency. Oyin, listen to me. I will explain everything to you on the plane. Just do as I say. We'll discuss all of this on the plane.

Yomi Nobody is getting on *any* plane; nobody is going to Port Harcourt!

Mrs O What do you mean nobody's going to Port Harcourt? Do you think I have packed up all these for nothing?

Yomi Yes! Yes, you have, Mummy! Nobody is going to Port Harcourt right now – well, at least, except maybe you, Mummy. It's a very long story. I can't explain everything right now, so let's just leave it as that for now. There will be no trips to Port Harcourt today.

Mrs O *(Eyes him with contained rage)* Oyin, hand me that bag. Amy, have you called the taxi?

Amy *(Meekly)* Yes . . . yes, Ma.

Oyin turns with exasperation to Yomi.

Yomi *(Takes a deep breath and raises his voice)* Mum, nobody is going to Port Harcourt because there isn't going to be any wedding!

Mrs O *(Whirls to face Amy)* You told him?

Amy *(Quickly)* No! No, I didn't!

Mrs O *(Shaking head quickly)* It doesn't matter. Oyin, hand me that bag now; we're leaving – all of us!

Yomi You're not listening, Mum.

Mrs O *(Sharply)* It is not a good time to question me. Just do as you're told!

Yomi *(Gaping)* You can't talk to me that way; I'm not a child!

Mrs O *(Muttering)* God help me!

Mrs O moves quickly, grabs a handle off the bag and tugs hard. Oyin restrains and between the two, the bag comes undone spilling its contents out. Amidst the clothes strewn on the floor, a litter of invitation cards are also exposed. With a gasp, Mrs O rushes to pick them; Amy rushes to join her, the others watch in confusion.

Yomi What are those?

Mrs O *(Quickly)* Just stay away, okay!

Oyin We need to tell her, Yomi! Tell her this is all a lie. Tell her. . . tell her there really isn't any wedding! Tell her everything now!

Oyin bends to gently help her mother and picks up a stray card.

Mrs O *(With odd fury)* I said stay away!

Oyin Mum, I think you should . . . calm down . . . and listen. There's something we need to tell you .

Oyin glances casually at the card as she reaches to hand it to Mother. The casual glance turns furtive as her eyes widen at its content.

Oyin *(With shock)* Uh?

Mrs O *(Looking up at Oyin, her expression enraged)* Didn't I ask you to stay away? Give me that!

She lunges for the card but Oyin steps back instinctively – still in a reel.

Yomi *(Moving quickly to Oyin's side)* What is that?

Yomi spies the content and lets off a gasp.

Yomi What is the meaning of this?

Amy looks everywhere except into Yomi's face. Mrs O's expression is enraged. Oyin is clearly perplexed.

Yomi *(With a roar)* Is this some kind of joke?

A prolonged silence

Yomi Mother?

Silence

Yomi *(Turning a lethal gaze to Amy)* Amy, what is this? Your name is on this wedding invitation card, so one of us must have an idea about what in heaven is going on?

Amy offers no response.

Yomi Answer me! Why are there wedding invitation cards with both our names on them?

Mrs O *(Nonchalantly)* Well . . . Now you know. It will save us the drama when we get home to Port Harcourt. Pick your bags, we are all leaving now!

Yomi I'm not leaving this house! Have you lost your mind?

Mrs O whirls and gives an instant slap to Yomi's cheek. Shocked and breathing fast with rage, he holds his bruised face.

Mrs O *(With contained authority)* Show some respect to your mother!
(With embittered finality)
Do I look like Talia, or any of the girls you have been messing around with?

There is a moment of pause.

Mrs O I am your mother! You will respect me and do what I ask of you!

Yomi and Oyin express profound shock.

A long silence.

Yomi *(Turning a furious glance to Amy)* You told her? You bastard!

Mrs O *(Shaking with rage)* If I were you, I'd be careful who you call a bastard! Your father would be turning in his grave!

Amy I didn't tell her . . . I promise you; I did not tell her!

Mrs O *(Shakes her head)* Is it now clear to you what is happening here? You are coming with me to Port Harcourt today.

Yomi *(Waving the invitation card wildly)* To do what? To get married to Amy, against my wishes?!

Mrs O Act like an animal and you will be treated like one!

Mrs O grabs the bag from Oyin and heads with it towards the exit.

Yomi You can't just bundle and marry me off like a slave? I'm a man – a grown man!

Mrs O *(Sarcastically)* Call your lawyers; ask them to sue me.

She exits.

Yomi *(Whirls to face Amy)* Did you know about this?

Amy Yomi, I . . .

Yomi Answer me! I said, did you know about this?

Amy It wasn't entirely my idea; I only agreed to help.

Yomi Is this a joke?

Amy No . . . no, it is not.
(After a brief hesitation, she speaks quickly) Your mother knows everything. The girls you have been seeing, the drinking and the drugs, the blackmail . . . She knows everything.

Yomi appears to take a moment to digest the new information.

Yomi And so what if she knows? I am a grown man. I can do whatever I want with my life!

Amy Pastor Yomi, you know this is not just about the girls. Your mother knows everything. She knows everything!

Yomi goes briefly quiet and appears to be panicking.

Yomi So, she intends that we get married? In Port Harcourt? Me and you?

Amy Yes. It has all been arranged. Both of our families have been informed.

Oyin I . . . I don't understand.

Yomi *(Wildly)* How long has this been going on?

Amy is quiet.

Yomi Answer my bloody questions!

Amy Two months ago. She started planning the wedding two months ago after she found out. Kike called your mother.

Oyin *(Shocked)* Two months? But . . . but what about all of these? The fake wedding story and all the lies?

Amy There is no *fake* wedding. Your Mother has been a part of it all from the beginning. The shopping, the invitation cards, the church service bookings – it's all real. The lies were all a smokescreen. Your mum is only here to tidy things up and . . . take us to Port Harcourt.

Yomi To get married to you?

Amy nods.

Oyin *(Drops weakly into a chair)* Oh-my-God!

In a quick gesture, Yomi crosses over and attempts to grab Amy violently, but Oyin moves quickly, and a struggle ensues between all three until Mrs O returns.

Mrs O Take your hands off her!

The three unentangle and Yomi stands looking wild.

Yomi I'm not going anywhere, *Mother!*

Mrs O You don't have a choice in this matter! God knows I'll tie you up with every strength I have left in me. I will drag you bound up into the plane if I have to! If you know what's good for you, you'll follow me quietly with whatever shred of dignity you have left.

Oyin *(Beseechingly)* Mummy, please . . . please calm down; calm down and let's talk about this.

Mrs O *(Emphatically)* Over my dead body! Do you hear that, Yomi? Over my dead body! You have a very small window to redeem whatever is left of your damned soul. My suggestion to you is that you take that opportunity and get on the plane quietly tonight. Otherwise, I promise you, I will ensure that all the fury of hell is unleashed on you for what you have done, Yomi! Your father will be turning in his grave!

She is suddenly overwhelmed with emotion and starts to cry.

Over my dead body! Your father will be turning in his grave, Yomi!

At that instant, a sober Kike walks in; all eyes turn to her.

Mrs O see her, crouches to the floor and breaks down into tears.

Yomi Mother please . . . I made a mistake . . . I made a terrible mistake.

Oyin *(Takes a deep, troubled breath)*
Kike . . . Kike, what is going on? What is going on? What have you done?

Kike *(Her voice cracks with emotion)* What have I done?
(Turns a sober face to her mother)
I'm pregnant. This is it. I'm pregnant, Mummy.

Mrs O Oh god, it is true! God help me, it is true!

Kike *(Appearing deeply broken)* Yes. Yes mummy, we are having a baby. I am so sorry.

Mrs O *(Shaking her head violently)* This is not your fault Kike! This is not your fault!

Yomi *(Wildly)* Stop it! Stop it, Kike!

Mrs O starts to wail loudly.

Oyin Kike, what is going on?

Kike *(Rubbing her tummy slowly)* The baby needs a home.
(Turns to Yomi)
Your daughter needs a home.

Oyin *(A look of horrified dawning)* Kike, what are you saying?
What are you saying, Kike?

(She turns to Yomi)
What is she saying?
Is this . . . Is this true, Yomi?

Yomi offers no response.

Oyin Oh my God. No! No!! No, Kike!!!

Amy moves and attempts to support Oyin, but she violently resists.

Oyin Yomi, answer me! Tell me this is not true!

Kike Mum knows everything. I have told mum everything. This outcome is the best way.

Oyin *(Wildly)* The best way? What are you saying Kike?

Kike It is the best way to quietly resolve this. You will all get on that flight to Port Harcourt. I will stay behind, here in Lagos. Yomi and Amy will get married and remain in Port Harcourt to prepare a home for his daughter – as far away as possible from attention. When the baby arrives, Mum will return to Lagos to collect the child and bring her to you. She will belong to both of you – Yomi and Amy. You will care for her like your own, and nobody will ever, ever find out the truth. The child must also never know the truth. She must never discover that she is the taboo result of night consumed by drunken recklessness and stolen vulnerability.
(Raises her voice with deep emotion and angst)
Do you hear me, Yomi? This child must never ever know! Promise me that!

Amy *(Moves close to support Kike)* I hear you, Kike. All that we have discussed – you have my word.

Oyin breaks out in tears.

Oyin *(Gasping desperately)* Oh my God, Kike! Oh my God!

Kike I will be going away when all of this is over. Mother, I have delivered my side of this bargain to you.
(With a pained whisper) Thank you.

Mrs O stutters speechlessly, then suddenly lunges towards Yomi with rage.

Mrs O You bastard!

SCENE ENDS.

SCENE NINE: STAND BY ME

Oyin is alone on stage to deliver a closing monologue.

Oyin *(Quietly)* For every one of us, one day, a raging storm will enter our lives, and it will disrespect all our daydreams.

This time last year, I watched, screamed, and cursed as unwelcome strangers entered our home. They sang and danced like mad men while our own hearts shattered as they placed that wooden box in the centre of our lives. Like a solid statement of fact – no more prayers to be said. Daddy was gone. I waited for Him to do something. I worried that maybe the lid was shut too tight, but he did not stir. Instead, we were stuck in what felt like an utterly surreal reality. A cruel end to all our hopes and expectations.

Loss changes you. It breaks and remakes you. After you have stood at the abyss, you understand frailty and mortality. You become scarred; you become scared because you fully understand that all of life is fleeting, like a daydream. You become wise; you become wild. I have pondered the maddening questions of why? And found them fruitless endeavours. I have hounded the doors of heaven and returned home to silence, a curious acknowledgment that sometimes everything will fall apart. This too, is supposed to be fine on the altars of doxology.

We don't really talk about grief. The one single thing that will screw all of us over. Maybe because it messes with our heads – makes us uncomfortable. So instead, we chime familiar platitudes – you will be fine, time will heal our wounds of loss, or at least, mask our brokenness. We cannot tidy up grief to make her pretty. She will elude you. It is supposed to be okay, but it is not. I am here; I am there; You are where? I am nowhere. Punched twice to the gut. It is complicated.

Don't get me wrong, the faith is there. It's not that I have stopped believing . . . but I am hurt and deeply disappointed with how He has dealt these cards. Maybe I have been waiting for explanations – maybe even an apology. Is it too much to ask?

On the day that our lives fall apart, I hope that our convictions will remain unyielding – that your faith does not get flung aside. I hope that you will make your best effort to do what is right and needful for the times into which we are called. When life calls, when everything falls apart, when all hell is breaking loose, I hope that you will not allow yourselves to fall to pieces. Instead, I hope that you will stand – broken and disappointed; but still standing.

One day a new chapter will turn; a new song will start to play. It will be different to all that you have known, but it will be beautiful – utterly beautiful in its own right. I hope that you will sing again. I hope you know that you will always be a part of me. I hope that you will pray for me, from wherever you are, a simple prayer...

Blessed are those who mourn. May God comfort their pain.

Don't tell Daddy what happened in Lagos.

BLACKOUT

THE END.

ABOUT THE AUTHOR

Yemi is a freelance writer, theatre, and cinema enthusiast.

His writings explore social commentary themes, faith, and light-hearted observations of human experiences. He has written stage plays, podcast serial, short stories, website content, and radio production.

When not immersed in his day job, he enjoys jazz nights and indulging daydreams of a carefree life sampling mocktails on a beach holiday.

Yemi is married and lives with his wife and two boys in London. Follow him on Instagram and twitter @podsixteen.